This igloo book

belongs to:

D0417190

....

igloobooks

Published in 2019
by Igloo Books Ltd
Cottage Farm
Sywell
NN6 0BJ
www.igloobooks.com

Copyright © 2018 Igloo Books Ltd
Igloo Books is an imprint of Bonnier Books UK

All rights reserved. No part of this publication may be
reproduced or transmitted in any form or by any means,
electronic, or mechanical, including photocopying, recording,
or by any information storage and retrieval system,
without permission in writing from the publisher.

0819 001.01
2 4 6 8 10 9 7 5 3 1
ISBN 978-1-83852-228-5

Written by Melanie Joyce
Illustrated by Steve James

Cover designed by Amy Bradford
Interiors designed by Amy Bradford & Alex Alexandrou
Edited by Kathryn Beer

Printed and manufactured in China

BUBBLEGUM
BEAR

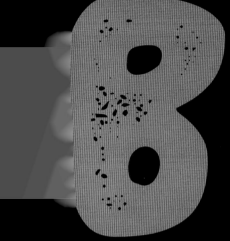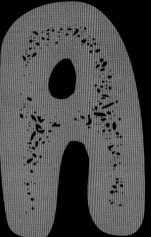

igloobooks

There's nobody quite like

Bubblegum Bear.

He's bubblegum pink

and he doesn't care.

Bubblegum isn't like his other bear friends.
He doesn't follow fashion or keep up with trends.

Bubblegum Bear
can't dance, or sing...

... but that doesn't matter,
he just does his own thing.

And even though it sounds like he might be in pain, everyone cheers and cries,

Please sing again!

Bubblegum Bear doesn't worry at all,
that he can't swing a racket, or score with a ball.

It doesn't bother him that he can't run fast,
and at the end of a race is usually last.

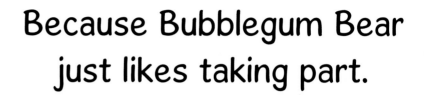

Because Bubblegum Bear
just likes taking part.

Whatever he does,
he gives it his heart.

And if things don't work out, well that is okay.

Bubblegum Bear won't let it spoil his day.

Big, swirly slide

If it's cloudy and dull, with rain pouring down,
Bubblegum Bear won't grumble or frown.

He'll put on his boots to play outside,
and all his friends follow to the big, swirly slide.

Bubblegum Bear never has any doubt,
that after the rain, the sun will come out.

He'll pack up some snacks and go on a hike...

... or maybe whizz off on his red, shiny bike.

Life should be fun!

... cries Bubblegum Bear, as he bounces up and down, and flies through the air.

Bubblegum Bear is as happy as can be,
playing at pirates, sailing out to sea!

And if Bubblegum's friends are feeling sad,
he hugs them and says,

They have so much fun playing happily together.

His friends think he is the best bear ever.

Bubblegum says,

There's nothing special about me.

But he has a gift that everyone can see.

Because Bubblegum cares
and is always kind, too.
So everyone says,

Bubblegum,
we love you!

Bubblegum Bear always does his best, and at the end of the day when it's time to rest...

... he sleeps peacefully because
there is no one to compare,

with the **lovely,**

cuddly, pink

Bubblegum

Bear.

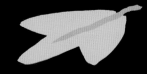